This book
belongs to

----- - - - - - - - -

For Mum and Dad, we travelled well.
CC

For Emma and Mark.
AS

Maggie's Magical Islands

Coo Clayton   Alison Soye

BLACK & WHITE PUBLISHING

Maggie and Mum love to explore.

They're getting ready for a holiday adventure when they discover an old map. Could it be a treasure map?

Est 1996
SCOTLANDS
Best B&Bs
Quality assured
Choose your perfect place to stay in Scotland
Edinburgh, UK
Sat, Sunny
16 °C | °F
9:00
12:00
17:00
SAT 16
SUN 12
MON 14
TUE
Shetland
Lewis
Inverness
Skye
Aberdeen
NORTH SEA
NORTH ATLANTIC OCEAN
Highland
Dundee
Mull
Edinburgh
Glasgow
Islay
Arran
Lowland
N
E
W
S
To do:
· Book ferry ✓
· Book place to stay
ROUND RICH TEA BISCUITS
ROUND RICH TEA BISCUITS

It's a map of the Scottish Islands!
And look, one of the islands has a big X on it.

Together Maggie and Mum plan a trip to visit
five different islands. Last stop: X marks the spot!
What will the mystery treasure be?

Maggie and Mum are so busy checking
ferry times and weather forecasts that . . . Oh no!
They've forgotten to book anywhere to stay.

'Don't worry, Mum,' Maggie says as they jump off the ferry
on to the Isle of Arran. 'Can you see what I see?'

'Perfect.' Mum claps her hands.
'That's our transport and beds sorted!'

Arran is an amazing island to explore in a campervan!
'Wow! How did this stone circle get here?'
Maggie asks as they trek across Machrie Moor.

'It's magical, isn't it?' Mum replies.
'Neolithic people built it nearly
5,000 years ago.'

But as they walk back to the campervan . . .

'Oh no! What's all that smoke?' Maggie asks.

'Looks like engine problems!' Mum says.
'Maybe we need a new way to travel or
we'll never find the treasure?'

'I love our new hire bikes!' Maggie yells
as she tests out her VERY loud bell.
'They are just what we need to explore
Islay, the Queen of the Hebrides!'

DISTILLERY

SINGING SANDS

Mum stops to check the map.
'This beach is the perfect spot to pitch our tent.
It's called the Singing Sands.'

But camping is too wild for Mum and Maggie!

'That was an awfully stormy night,' Mum says.
'Get the map out, Maggie. Let's find somewhere with
a proper roof and a comfy bed.'

The faithful ferry takes Maggie and Mum onwards to the Isle of Mull and ever closer to the treasure. The wind is blowing a hoolie and the waves are choppy.

'What a bumpy ride,' Mum yawns.
'Whatever next?'

Maggie spots a grand castle with
her binoculars. 'I'm sure we'll get a great
night's sleep there,' she tells Mum.

'What's that spooky noise?'
Maggie clutches Mum in the middle of the night.
'Is it a ghost?'

'Shh now,' Mum reassures her.
'It's just the wind whistling through the windows.'

But Maggie's not so sure.
'I don't like this haunted castle. Let's look at the map
and get going as soon as we can.'

FAIRY POOLS

Now Maggie and Mum are on the Isle of Skye.

'My legs are SO tired,' Maggie grumbles.
'When will these glens ever end?'

'Here,' Mum says. 'At the magical fairy pools –'

'Look at me!' Maggie cries, splashing in the clear water.
She wades in a little, looking for fairies.
'It's f-f-f-freezing,' she gasps, as she jumps out again.

They find a cosy wee bothy to sleep in. Mum makes a fire and
Maggie hangs her swimming costume up to dry.

Her dreams are full of treasure. She can't wait to find it tomorrow!

The next day, Maggie and Mum cycle
to the top of the Isle of Lewis.

'I can see a lighthouse,' Mum calls out.
'It's marked with an X on the map.
But I can't see any treasure.'

'Do you know where the treasure is?' Maggie asks the lighthouse keeper.

'Aye, the treasure is right here,' he says with a smile. 'But you'll need to wait until after dark to see it!'

Maggie and Mum are SO lucky!
They're spending the night in the lighthouse.

'But don't fall asleep,' the lighthouse keeper warns Maggie.
'Because when it gets dark, the treasure will appear . . .'

'Wow! Wow! WOW!' Maggie can't believe her eyes.

Shimmering waves of light are sweeping across the sky.

'The Northern Lights,' Mum tells her.
'See how they fill the night with colour.'

'It's like an amazing dance in the sky,' Maggie whispers sleepily. 'What a magical end to our island adventures.'

I'm hiding in each scene - can you spot me?

First published 2020
by Black & White Publishing Ltd
Nautical House, 104 Commercial Street, Edinburgh, EH6 6NF

1 3 5 7 9 10 8 6 4 2   20 21 22 23

ISBN: 978 1 78530 314 2

Text copyright © Coo Clayton 2020
Illustrations copyright © Alison Soye 2020

Printed in India by Replika Press